DAVE

Pigeon

For Serena,
Happy birthday to my
favourite writer.
S.H.

For Uncle Kieran,
S.D.

First published in 2017
by Faber and Faber Limited
Bloomsbury House
74–77 Great Russell Street
London WC1B 3DA

Designed by Faber and Faber
Printed and bound in the UK by
CPI Group (UK) Ltd, Croydon, CR0 4YY

Text © Swapna Haddow, 2017
Illustrations © Sheena Dempsey, 2017

A CIP record for this book is available from the British Library

ISBN/978-0-571-32443-9

2 4 6 8 10 9 7 5 3 1

DAVE
Pigeon's
book on

How Not to Get Plucked, Minced, Roasted and Served Up with Ketchup

Typed up by Skipper whilst
Swapna Haddow
had a nap.

Illustrated by
Sheena Dempsey
because Dave Pigeon lost his felt tip pens.

FABER & FABER

This book is in Pigeonese. The following words are to test if you can read Pigeonese:

Cats

Smell

Of

Farts

And

Cabbage

Could you read all the words? Are you sure? Do you want to try that fourth word again?

If you managed to read the words on this page, you will have no problem understanding the Pigeonese in this book. You may turn the page . . .

. . . NOW

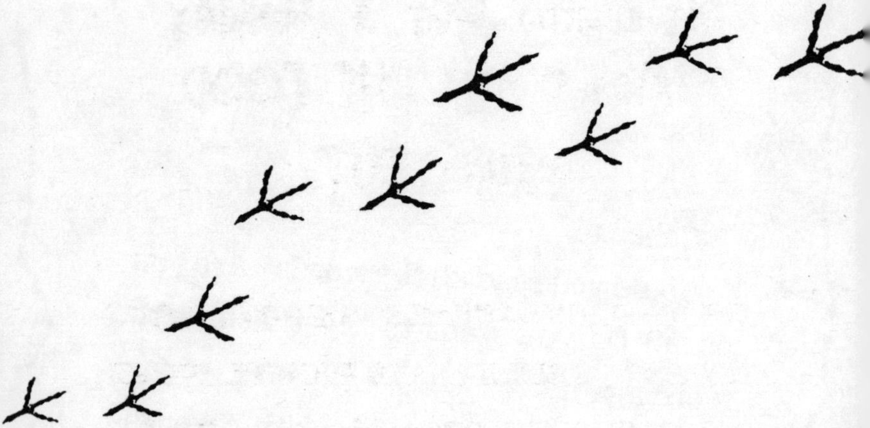

1
It Turns Out a 'Holiday' Means ALL THE FOOD RUNS OUT

WE'RE BACK! IT'S ME, SKIPPER, WITH MY BEST FRIEND DAVE PIGEON. WE'RE A BIT SHOUTY BECAUSE THE HUMAN LADY'S NEXT-DOOR NEIGHBOUR, HIM NEXT DOOR, HAS THE LEAF BLOWER ON.

Thank Pigeon for that. He's stopped. I could barely hear myself flap.

OH NO! THERE HE GOES AGAIN. I DON'T UNDERSTAND WHY HE HAS TO SING SO LOUDLY TOO.

IS THAT WHAT THE HUMANS CALL SINGING? I THOUGHT HIS ARM HAD FALLEN OFF AND HE WAS SCREAMING FOR HELP.

THIS leaf BLOWER is DRIVING me QUACKERS!

WE ARE NEVER GOING TO FINISH WRITING THE BOOK WITH THIS RACKET.

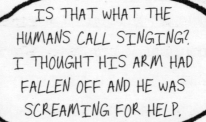

Why are you still shouting, Dave? The leaf blower has stopped.

IT'S REALLY HARD TO STOP SHOUTING ONCE YOU'VE STARTED.

Despite the terrible singing, and the leaf-blowing, which is completely ridiculous because that is what the wind is for, Him Next Door is our hero. We owe him our lives.

Normally, Dave would have sent me over the fence to kick a stone up the machine. But not today. Him Next Door screeching at the top of his lungs and the

mmmmeeeeehhhhh mmmmeeeeehhhhh mmmmeeeeehhhhh from the garden vacuum cleaner was as magnificent as finding an entire unopened packet of salty crisps.

You see, Him Next Door saved our beaks, and it all started—

HAVE YOU STARTED THE STORY YET?

I'm just about to! By the way, you are still shouting.

SORRY.

It started with the Human Lady's 'holiday'.

That morning, she'd come over to our shed at the end of her garden with an entire loaf still in its bag. I could smell her evil pet, Mean Cat, lurking behind. Me and Dave stayed high on the rickety window ledge in case the fuzzball tried to spring at us.

'Don't worry, you can come down,' the Human Lady said, once she was safely inside the shed. 'I've left that mean cat in the garden.'

Dave jumped from the ledge first. He landed on the worktop by the door and the Human Lady scooped him up.

She nodded at me. 'And you too.'

I swooped down, a dark grey blush rising over my face as she grinned and threw some torn bread for me to peck at.

'I have some news,' she said to us. 'I'm going on a little holiday.'

'What's a "holiday"?' I asked Dave, in a low coo.

'I think it's a type of horse.'

'Something is wrong with my cat,' the Human Lady continued. 'She's been awfully jittery recently . . .'

Me and Dave stopped eating and looked at each other. We then turned back to the Human Lady and tried our best to look innocent and not at all like we knew *anything* about what might have made Mean Cat feel awfully jittery recently.

Remember our first book?

It was the book where I heroically got rid of Mean Cat.

where WE heroically got rid of Mean Cat.

After she destroyed my wing . . .
Because we were attacked by a gang of a thousand ninja fire-breathing eagles.
But we had to bring her back . . .
It was more like a hundred very annoying birds from the local neighbourhood, Dave.
Bringing back Mean Cat got rid of the irritating birds and life went back to normal. I do remember writing a chapter about how Mean Cat returned, but somehow those last pages disappeared . . .
DAVE
Skipper, I had to get rid of those pages. My grandma bought that book. I couldn't have her knowing we needed help from a cat.

'I'm going to take her away to relax a bit,' the Human Lady continued. 'The way she's been jumping around, you'd think she'd been shot out of a cannon or something.'

We gave the Human Lady our best 'we have no idea about no cannon' eyes.

She bent down to rub the top of my head and mentioned something about 'a few days away' as she squished the feathers over my ears.

'What did she say?' I asked Dave as the Human Lady swung the shed door shut behind her.

'She's going on holiday, whatever *that* is.'

'Not that bit,'

I said. 'It was something about being away.'

'Weren't you listening?'

'She was stroking me. It's hard to hear anything when your ear holes are blocked by Human hands.'

Dave shook his head. 'Well, I wasn't listening. It was your turn to listen.'

I stopped pecking at the stale crumbs and looked at Dave. In the space of about thirty seconds, he'd eaten almost half the bread the Human Lady had given us. Dave was now relaxed, slouched back on his bottom, letting the tiny crumbs trapped on his chest feathers tumble down his wing into a bready heap.

But I couldn't shake the feeling that something was wrong. My insides felt like blancmange and my legs wouldn't stop trembling.

'Aren't you hungry?' Dave asked.

'No.'

'Lunch will be out soon,' Dave said, curling up for a nap. 'I'm sure it'll be croissants today.' His eyelids began to droop, and his coos slurred to snores. 'Wake me when the food arrives,' he mumbled.

I jumped up to the window ledge and looked out across the garden. Coming towards the shed was a flying ball of yellow and gold feathers.

TINKLES.

I looked for somewhere to hide, but Him Next Door's nosy pet canary had spotted me.

'Yoo hoo!' she whistled.

Tinkles landed on the ledge and waited

for me to join her outside the shed. Her
pink beak had just had its weekly shine at
the vet's, and her talons had a fresh coat of
sparkly nail varnish. I still hadn't forgiven
her for being part of the gang who tried to
steal our biscuits, but Dave was asleep and
there wasn't much else to do until lunch.

'Hello, Tinkles,' I said, squeezing out
under the window.

'I just came over to say goodbye to you boys,' she chirped.

'Are you leaving for ever?' I asked, hopefully.

'No,' she said, shaking her head. 'I thought you'd be off, now the Human Lady has left.'

'What are you tweeting on about?'

Tinkles laughed, her voice like a thousand high-pitched bells. 'I saw the Human Lady pack her bags and leave with her cat this morning.'

'She wouldn't leave us,' I said.

Tinkles peered through the shed window. Dave was dozing against the half-eaten loaf of bread.

'Looks like that's the last of your food

supplies.' She smirked. 'I best be off. *My* Human has just bought me a personalised birdbath to sit in. It makes its own bubbles.'

She took off from the shed. I could hear her chirping all the way across the fence back to Him Next Door.

Tinkles couldn't have been right about the Human Lady, could she? Surely our Human Lady wouldn't leave us?

The house seemed very quiet.

Something was wrong.

I paced the length of the ledge, then when I was sure Mean Cat wasn't in the garden, I kicked off from the shed window and flew down to the Human Lady's house.

I looked through the windows. The Human Lady wasn't there. I listened for the familiar purrs and scratching of Mean Cat. Nothing. The windows were shut tight and the back door was locked.

I landed by the cat flap.

I pushed hard – and fell back on my bottom.

I pushed again. And again. First with my head, then my feet, then my sore bottom.

The cat flap was bolted shut.

No matter how hard I shoved and pecked and kicked, the flap wouldn't budge.

'What are you doing?' Dave called out

from across the garden.

I looked up at the house. 'I think the Human Lady has gone.'

Dave flapped madly and hopped across the lawn, heaving his stomach over the steps as it wobbled, full of bread. His Medal of the Brave, an old bottle top that was stuck to his chest with a piece of chewing gum, twisted and dangled as he tripped over his own feet, running towards the house.

'Where is she?' His eyes were wide and

panicked as he arched his head and bashed at the cat flap. 'Check the windows.'

Fluttering back up to the window ledge, I peered in. The entire house was dark. The telly was off. Even the washing machine wasn't whirring round and round.

I couldn't sense our Human Lady anywhere.

'She's left us.' Dave dropped down into a feathery heap. 'There'll be no more food.'

'Maybe she's popped to the shops?'

'She never takes Mean Cat to the shops,' Dave squawked. 'She's GONE.'

I collapsed down next to Dave. Heavy grey clouds had started to gather in the sky. The paving stones felt cold and the broken flowerpots looked more broken.

Our Human Lady had left us and we were all alone.

No more tickles under my beak. No more nuzzles on the top of my head. No more Human Lady smiles just for me.

We had been abandoned.

The end of the book.

This really is the end of the book. There's no more story left. The end.

I'm not kidding. It's The Actual End.

(The endy endy end end endy endy end. Endy endy endy endy endy endy end.)

THE END.

Skipper, I don't think the pages are in the right order.

Sorry, readers.
Here's the second
chapter.

2

The Man with the Umbrellas

'What are we going to do?' I wailed.

Dave sat up. His lower beak stuck out a
bit as he tried hard not to cry. He put his
good wing around me. 'We are going to find
ourselves another Human.'

'I just don't believe that the Human Lady
would leave us,' I pleaded.

'Well, she has,' Dave said. 'It's time to move on.'

'It doesn't make any sense. She gave us a shed.'

I looked at our shed. How could I say goodbye to our wobbly shelves and the comfy old paint-tin lids that we slept in? And then there was my typewriter . . .

'Let's go, Skipper! Stop moping around.'

I followed my best friend up on to the

washing line, where he spied out over the long row of gardens.

'Shall we try Him Next Door?' I asked.

'No point. He's got a full house with his irritating canary.' Dave craned his neck further forwards and stared across the fences. 'Follow me.'

We fluttered down from the washing line and headed towards the back of the garden. Dave pushed his way through the flapping wood panels of the broken fence and held them apart as I squeezed through.

We had to walk as Dave's wing was still too damaged to fly. As my friend charged on, I secretly looked back at the Human Lady's garden, and cooed a tiny goodbye to our lovely home.

Dave hopped along the track behind the gardens. His head bobbed as he stopped at each new fence, trying to find a crack in the wood or a clearing in the hedge to squeeze through and spy on each potential new home.

'Too many cats,' he announced if he saw

the slightest hint of a cat flap.

'Not enough biscuits to go around,' he declared if he saw swings and slides in the garden for Little Humans.

'Too boring,' he exclaimed, his beak all twisted in disgust, if he couldn't see a telly through the glass of the patio.

My legs were aching and my wings were sore from scraping my way through prickly hedgerows and splintered fences. We'd walked past at least seventeen houses when Dave finally stopped and decided it was time for lunch. My stomach had been growling ever more loudly and angrily since house four.

'Let's go back,' I said.

'To what?' Dave said, pecking through

a pile of crisp brown leaves, looking for something to eat. He slumped down in a heap. His feet disappeared under his feathers and his head crumpled into his neck. 'Nobody wants us,' he wailed. 'I miss biscuits.'

'Don't worry, Dave.' I looked at my distraught friend. 'Remember there was a time before the Human Lady and we were just fine.'

'"Fine"?' Dave spat. 'Who wants to be "just fine"?' He sank further into his feathered belly. 'I don't want to go back to scratching around under benches and hunting through abandoned picnic baskets. I want to live in a shed with a constant supply of bread—'

'Shush.'

'Don't shush me,' Dave said, indignantly. 'I need to get this rant off my chest feathers—'

'Shush!'

'How dare you—'

'Dave,' I squawked. 'Can't you hear that?'

'I can't hear anything over your shushing.'

'Stop talking and listen!'

There, carried on the air, over the fence, was the sound of a Human clucking. That sucking-in-on-the-teeth thing that every Human does when they are trying to call an animal towards them. Especially when they want to share food.

'Heeeeere, pijjy pigeons.'

'Did you hear that?' I said, jumping up.

'What's a "pijjy"?' Dave said.

'Us, you catbrain!'

'Heeeeere, pijjy pigeons.' The call came again, in a deep scratchy voice. 'Come here, little pigeons.'

'Did you hear that?' Dave cried, bouncing back on to his feet. 'That Human is calling for us pijjies!'

We leapt across the path and darted towards the sound of crushed stale bread dropping on to the ground, as the call for pigeons got louder.

'This is the house,' Dave said, skipping up and down.

He used his head to carve out a space in the hedge, and then launched his body forward.

'Help me!'

Dave was stuck deep in the hedge.

His head was poking through the leaves into the garden of the calling Human, but his bottom was still sticking out, dangling over the path. His skinny pink legs kicked mid-air in the middle of the hedge.

OK, OK. I think they get the picture. Let's move on.

In case you haven't, here's a drawing.

I headbutted Dave's bottom through the hedge and jumped forwards hard, shoving us both into the garden. We rolled out of the green leaves and twigs and landed in a patch of overgrown grass and weeds.

The garden was thick and wild. Not at all like the Human Lady's. The white wispy heads of old dandelions prickled my beak. The grass was long, yellow and spiky. Thick, tangled, thorny weeds scratched my legs as I picked my feet up to dodge the maze of fox droppings and rotten, fallen fruit. There was a rusty washing machine and a mangled shopping trolley lying on its side to our left, and a smelly pile of bulging rubbish bags to our right.

'I'm not sure about this place,' I said to Dave.

He looked around. 'It's fine, Skipper.'

'We could just keep looking for another Human . . .'

Another scattering of breadcrumbs pattered over the lawn.

'I'm too hungry to look for someone else!' Dave charged towards the Human house and the sound of the crumbs. My stomach roared, threatening to eat my own insides, so I chased after my friend.

'Here! Here, pijjy pijjies,' the call came again.

We looked up to find a Human standing in the long grass. He was a tall skinny Man, and he was covered head to toe in

a dirty yellow plastic mac that creaked
and squeaked every time he reached into
his pocket and pulled out more crushed
bread. Even his
legs and feet
were covered
in yellow
plastic. He looked
like a Human
shopping bag.

'This is it, Skipper,'
Dave sang, diving
head first into a
pile of bread
scraps.
'This is our
new home.'

'That's right, pigeons, eat up,' the Human Man said.

His voice was cold, and sounded like pigeon claws scraping along a metal park bench. His eyes were pale – almost as pale as the whites of his eyeballs – and a thin flap of silver wiry hair peeked out from under his hood.

But it wasn't just his chilling voice and ice-cold glare that sent a shudder up through my feathers.

On each of the Human Man's plastic-covered shoulders was a tiny umbrella, in matching yellow plastic. As soon as he had spotted us, he'd reached up to each shoulder and popped a clasp. Up shot the umbrellas. All the while the Human Man never once blinked as he stared us down.

'Dave . . .' I started. 'Did you see him open up those tiny umbrellas as soon as we got close to him?'

'Yes. Maybe he just doesn't like his shoulders getting wet in the rain?'

I looked up at the bright blue sky. The grey clouds had blown east, and there wasn't a single one above our heads.

'I'm really not sure about this Human.'

Dave stopped pecking. 'Skipper, I know you miss the Human Lady, but she's moved on. And it's time we did too.'

'Here you go,' the Human Man said, hurling a wedge of bread towards me.

Dave leapt towards the bread in the long grass.

The Human Man shrieked as Dave dived close to him. He stumbled over the tangled nettles as he backed away from Dave, chucking breadcrumbs as far away from himself as he could. He clutched his chest. His chin trembled as he tried to stop bread falling from his hands.

My friend turned back towards me, unsure.

'I don't think he wants us here,' I said.

'Wait,' the Human Man called out. 'No need to be afraid!'

It was hard to tell if he was trying to reassure us or himself.

3
Reginald Grimster Introduces Reginald Grimster

The Human Man threw out another handful of bread and Dave hopped up and raced forward, following the trail of stale crumbs, eager to jump into the Human's hand.

'No!' The hand whipped back into the plastic mac pocket at lightning speed.

Dave stopped and took a step back.

'See?' I said, pulling Dave away from the house. 'He doesn't want us here.'

'No, no! I meant "No, don't go!"' the Man panicked. 'Come on in, little pigeons.'

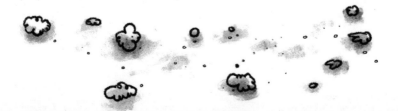

Dave shrugged me off. 'Don't get your tail feathers in a fluff, Skipper. He's asking us to come in.'

'Reginald Grimster wants you to come in,' the Man said.

'See?' Dave said to me.

Breadcrumbs showered down on top of us as the Human threw out handful after handful of the stuff. 'Reginald Grimster has more food inside,' he said.

'Who's Reginald Grimster?' Dave asked me as he craned his neck trying to look behind the Man.

'I think it's him,' I replied, nodding at the monogrammed pocket of the man's plastic mac. It was emblazoned with a swirly 'R' and 'G'.

Reginald Grimster continued to back his way towards the house. His bottom hit a closed patio door, and he slid his hand behind himself to slide the glass door open. He didn't once break eye contact with us.

'Come here, pijjy pijjies,' he blurted, as he continued to toss a breadcrumb path for us to follow into his house.

'I really don't have a good feeling about this,' I whispered.

Dave kicked me forward towards the darkened patio doors. 'Maybe he's not quite as nice as the Human Lady, and so far he's not too keen on petting us, but at least he'll keep us fed.'

'Reginald Grimster has lots of food here for you,' Reginald Grimster called out from inside his house.

'Besides, I have a great feeling about this,' Dave said, his beak curving up into a smirk.

My stomach knotted and my knees felt like melting ice cream, but I followed my friend as he pecked his way towards the house.

'This way, pijjies,' Reginald Grimster's voice came.

We hopped over the patio doorframe and into a dark dining room. The light from the windows caused long shadows to fall over a plastic-covered metal dining table and two plastic chairs tucked neatly underneath it. There was a cupboard in the corner stacked full of books. I waddled towards the cupboard. If this was going to be our new home I wanted to make sure there was a typewriter.

'Not there, pijjy!' Reginald Grimster barked at me. He hurried over and stood in my path, shielding the cupboard from me. I couldn't be sure, but I thought I saw two entire shelves of cookbooks peeking out from behind his legs.

'Skipper, don't upset Reginald.' Dave shook his head at me. 'He's our Human now.'

Dave jumped and half-flapped as he followed Reginald Grimster across the dining hall and into a small boxroom in the corner.

'Here, pijjy,' the man clucked at me, beckoning me over.

I followed after Dave. 'I wish he would stop calling me "pijjy".'

'Stop being such a misery-beak,' Dave said. 'He's just trying to be nice.'

The boxroom had been set up like a pet shop. There were tons of cages and birdhouses of all different shapes and sizes hanging from the ceiling. It was almost as

if Reginald Grimster was expecting us. On a long table lay a tray of sawdust and a trough of birdseed.

'Birdseed?' I shook my head. 'I thought you said you hated birdseed because it tastes like cardboard?'

Dave did seem briefly disappointed. 'It's no shed at the Human Lady's,' he said, uncertain. 'But it's a constant supply of food and somewhere for us to sleep. And I'm so hungry right now, cardboard will have to do.'

'Make yourselves at home, pijjies,' Reginald Grimster said. 'And make sure you eat up. Reginald Grimster wants you to eat up.'

He opened a huge bag of seed and filled

the trough to the top.

'You coming?' Dave cooed, bouncing off towards the trough.

'No thanks.'

'If you're off to do a bit of exploring, can you have a look for a kitchen and see what other food there is?' He scooped up a beakful of seed and swallowed it down. 'And add jammy biscuits to his shopping list if there aren't any.'

A phone rang in another room. I watched Reginald Grimster march out towards the sound. Dave was head-deep in the trench and didn't hear me as I left the room.

I went back out into the dining room

and followed the sound of the ringing phone. The kitchen would have to wait. I needed to find out more about Reginald Grimster.

He had turned down a corridor towards a noisy front room, where a television blared and flashed pictures of cooking programmes. The floor shook by the telly as he stomped up the staircase.

The ringing stopped. I could hear Reginald Grimster talking, so I flew up the stairs to the landing. I followed the sound of his voice to a small bathroom at the end of a short corridor. And there, in the reflection of the mirror, I saw Reginald Grimster gluing a silvery bush of hair on to his head.

Hair?

It was silver and hairy.

That would be a nest then.

Why would anyone glue a nest to their head?

So they wouldn't forget where they put it.

It was HAIR, Dave!

Reginald Grimster ruffled the newly glued hair on his head and gave himself a smirk in the mirror.

Reginald Grimster had a telephone nestled between his ear and his shoulder and was nodding along as he listened to the person on the other end.

'Oh yes,' he said into the telephone. 'It's all coming together nicely. Reginald Grimster found a really fat one today. It even came with a skinny little friend.'

There was silence for a moment as he listened.

'Hee hee hee,' Reginald Grimster laughed back into the receiver. His voice, scratchier and more crackly, made me shudder. 'I'm glad you asked. It's nuggets,' he said. 'Reginald Grimster is going to make pigeon nuggets.'

I did not start an argument.

You did.

Didn't.

See? You're doing it again.

Read this next bit and see for yourself who started the argument.

Reginald Grimster's words rang in my ears. I escaped down the stairs before he could spot me. A fat one and a skinny one? Was he talking about Dave and me?

I caught a glimpse of myself in the hallway mirror. It had been almost a day without any croissants or biscuits with the jammy bit in the middle. I suppose I did look a little skinnier than usual.

Well, I'm not the fat one. This is all muscle and feathers.

I swooped back through to the dining room and to the cupboard Reginald Grimster hadn't let me look at. High on the top shelf was a row of shiny silver keys. Beneath, stacked on two shelves, was cookbook after cookbook. Short ones, crumpled ones, leathery ones, ones

with bookmarks poking out of the top, and one that was held together with sticky tape and staples.

I fluttered close to the bottom shelf and squinted to read the titles in the shadows: *How to Fatten Up a Bird; How to Pluck a Bird; How to Roast a Bird; How to Make Nuggets from Any Bird You Find – and I Mean Any Bird, Like, Even a Bird You Lure into Your Garden with Breadcrumbs; How to Make Ice Cream (To Eat After Your Nuggets).*

'Dave!' I shrieked. 'Get in here!'

'I'm sleeping . . .' Dave's coo came back.

'Get in here NOW!'

A drowsy but cheerful Dave dragged his bulging belly through to the dining room. 'Why did you wake me up?'

'Dave, we need to get out of here.'

'Don't be ridiculous,' Dave snapped. 'I know it's not croissants and chocolate digestives but have you seen how much pigeontastic birdseed there is? And it's all ours!' Dave shook his head and started to turn back towards the feed room.

'Look at all these cookbooks!' I squawked at him.

Dave glanced up. 'So he's interested in cooking. Maybe he's a chef. What's wrong with that?'

'Don't you see a common theme?'

'Cooking?'

'Cooking *what*?' I said, pointing at every spine. Each had the word "Bird" on it.

'Cooking . . . books?'

'Dave!' My feathers were trembling. I slammed my wing down on the shelf. 'I think something very bad is going to happen to us. I think Reginald Grimster is going to turn us into pigeon nuggets. I heard him say so on the telephone!'

'Skipper, you're upset about the Human Lady. I understand. But you can't go around making things up.'

'I'm. Not.' I glared at Dave. 'We *need* to get out of here. The Human Man is dangerous.'

'Stop being so mean about Reginald Grimster.'

'I'm trying to save us,' I said through gritted beak.

'No,' Dave said. 'You are trying to start an argument.'

'But—'

'You go if you want to, but I'm staying here.'

'Fine.'

'Fine!'

'There you are, pijjies,' Reginald Grimster said just at that moment, stepping into the dining room. 'What are you doing in here?'

'I was just leaving,' I said.

Reginald Grimster didn't say anything back because he couldn't understand Pigeonese, but he flapped his hands from a distance and shooed Dave back towards the feed room. 'There you go, pijjy,' he said. 'You've got lots of eating up to do.'

'And you think this lovely Human wants to eat us?' Dave cooed over his shoulder at me. 'He just wants us to be happy and fed.'

'I'm going back to the shed, if you want to come.'

'No, thank you,' Dave chirped. 'Enjoy not having any food.'

Reginald was so busy pushing Dave back into the little boxroom, he didn't see me slip into the shadows of the dining room and back out into the garden.

I couldn't believe how catbrained Dave was being. I didn't want to leave him, but he gave me no choice. We needed to get out of that house. And it wasn't just because I missed the Human Lady and the way she smelled of grapefruit and bread, even though I wanted more than anything at that moment to be scooped up into her hands and stroked gently.

Pacing around the garden, I grew more and more furious at Dave. I kicked out at the long weeds, sending dandelion seeds crashing about me. Dave was supposed to

be my best friend. Some friend he'd turned
out to be. I smashed at the grass, crushing
the sharp, hard tips with my feet.

Dave was constantly choosing food over
me. This was just like the time he sent me to
get cheese from a mouse hole, even though
I was too big to squeeze through and I told
him I would get stuck. Which I did.

That wasn't my fault.

And the time he made me fly through the window of a school kitchen to swipe some sticky toffee pudding, and three dinner ladies and a head teacher chased me out whilst trying to bash me over the head with frying pans and metal ladles.

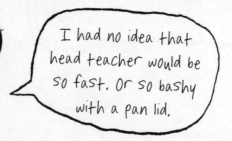

I had no idea that head teacher would be so fast. Or so bashy with a pan lid.

And then there was the time—

OK, OK. I'm sorry. What more do you want me to say?

Say sorry for starting the argument.

OK. I'm sorry you started the argument.

Dave!

Fine. I'm sorry we argued. And it might have been a tiny bit more my fault than yours.

That's better.

I was so furious with Dave. I needed to get away from that horrid house.

I flew up on to the fence to look over the gardens. The Human Lady's lopsided

kitty weathervane spun on its spoke in the distance. I was going home with or without Dave. I looked back at Reginald Grimster's house one last time before I set off, squawking a 'goodbye' as I glided up high into the sky.

5
The Toilet Brush Knocking at the Window

Tap. Tap.

A shadow at an upstairs window of Reginald Grimster's house caught my eye.

Tap. Tap. Tap.

The blurred grey rounded head of a toilet brush appeared to be knocking at the window for my attention.

I flew closer.

Tap. Tap. Tap. Tap. Tap. Tap. Tap. Tap. Tap. Tap. Tap.

'Are you OK, Toilet Brush?' I asked.

'I'm not a toilet brush, you nestbrain,' a voice cawed back.

'Who are you?'

'I'm fine.'

'No,' I said. 'Who are you? What's your name?'

'Fine.'

'No,' I said again. 'Not *how* are you. *Who* are you?'

'Fine!' the voice cried back. 'I'm fine.'

'OK.' I wanted to leave. 'I'm going. Glad you're OK.'

'It's spelled F-I-E-N-N-E!' the voice shrieked. 'My name is Fienne!'

'Ohhh,' I exclaimed. 'I'm Skipper.'

'How do you do, Skipper?'

'I'm fine.'

'I thought you were Skipper?' the voice replied, suspicious. '*I'm* Fienne.'

'Never mind,' I said. 'I'm off now.'

'You can't go!' the voice screeched. 'You need to get me out of here.'

'I've just had a feather-blazing row with my friend,' I explained. 'I told him I'm leaving, so I kind of have to leave in order to prove my point.'

'This is a matter of life or death. We are all in danger!'

'We?'

'Can you open this window and come inside?' Fienne said, his voice urgent. 'It's very hard to balance on a toilet seat when your leg is trapped.'

The window was slightly open. I wedged

my foot through the small gap at the bottom of the frame and shimmied across, wiggling my beak, then my head, then my neck through as the window slowly creaked open, letting me in.

'Fienne?' I whispered, once I'd squeezed through. It was the same bathroom where I had seen Reginald Grimster gluing hair

to his head. I spun up
and on to my feet,
kicking over a can
of air freshener
and sending it tumbling
into a roll of toilet paper.

'Fienne?'

'I'm here.'

Beneath the window
shelf, dangling upside
down from a string
attached to the
flush, was a
pigeon. His leg
was raw and
bruised where
the twine was

wrapped tightly around his ankle.

'Skipper, my leg is badly hurt,' he said. 'Can you peck me free?'

He swung from the thick string. As I struck it with my beak, it shredded. Eventually Fienne pulled away, breaking the cord, and collapsed on to the floor in a heap of feathers.

'Thank Pigeon you're here,' he said, limping as he got to his feet. 'You need to help me release the others.'

'Others?'

'My leg is too injured to complete this mission on my own. Can you help me?' Fienne shook the dirt from the bathroom floor off his feathers. He was a slim pigeon, with neatly trimmed, slick dark feathers

and what appeared to be a black ankle cuff with the letters 'S', 'P' and 'Y' printed on it in silver.

'Mission?' I said. 'What mission?'

'Top-secret pigeon business, I'm afraid.' His voice was no longer squeaky and panicked. It had slipped to a deep 'I'm important' tone. 'We need to move. Our position has been compromised.'

'I'm actually on my way back to my old home. I'm storming away from an argument with my friend Dave, remember?'

'Dave Pigeon?'

'You know Dave?'

'Everyone knows Dave,' Fienne said. 'I came across a copy of his first book last year.' He staggered towards me. 'You do know that Dave is in great danger, don't you?'

My throat went dry. 'What's going to happen to Dave?'

'Top-secret pigeon business, I'm afraid,' Fienne said. 'Follow me.'

Fienne wobbled forward, wincing as he limped on. He grabbed my wing and we tottered towards the bathroom door. 'We need to stay close so the Human doesn't see us.'

'Where are we going?' I asked.

'Top-secret pigeon business, I'm afraid.'

'What exactly did you mean by "Dave is in great danger"?'

'Top-secret—'

'"Pigeon business, I'm afraid"?' I finished, crossing my wings in front of my chest. I sighed, frustrated with all the secrets.

Fienne tutted at me, then held a single feather up to his beak. We fell silent. He stuck his head out from behind the bathroom doorframe and flicked his neck left and right before nodding at me and pushing me into the corridor.

He leaned against me for support and directed me down the corridor towards a shut door at the end of the hallway. Every time we heard a scrape or creak, he nudged us back into the shadows, where we stayed still, and all

I could see was the orange glow of his eyes.

We reached the door and Fienne knocked at it twice with his beak. Then once. Then three times. And then once again.

The sound of a coo followed by two short knocks came back.

Fienne cooed back and then farted.

'Sorry,' he said to me. 'That additional sound means we have to do the code again.'

'What code?'

'You're not meant to know anything about the code . . .' he said, his eyes narrowing. 'It's top-secret.'

'You were the one who just told me you were doing a code!'

'This is top-secret pigeon business, I'm afraid. You shouldn't have been listening.'

'But I can see you doing a code.'

'So stop watching,' he said.

I sighed and shut my eyes. I heard Fienne knock at the door with his beak twice. Again. Then once. Again. Then three times. Again. And then once again. Again.

The sound of a coo followed by two short knocks came back. Again.

And Fienne cooed back.

The door opened, and Fienne poked me towards the opening.

We went through.

6
Meanwhile . . .

Dave was eating birdseed.

7
Back to the Top-secret-Pigeon-Business-I'm-Afraid Room

Every inch of the room was filled with cages of pigeons. Row upon row of stacked coops covered the floor, shelves and cupboards. Inside each padlocked prison were pigeons, crammed tight, squished against the metal cage bars. There were hundreds upon hundreds of pigeons. And every frightened eye was on me and Fienne.

'What is this place?' I squawked.

Fienne looked at me.

'OK, OK,' I said. 'It's top-secret pigeon business. I get it.'

'Actually, this bit isn't top-secret,' a small voice chimed in. 'The Human with the tiny umbrellas on his shoulders has trapped us, and he intends to turn us all into pigeon nuggets.'

Every single pigeon started screeching. Wings beat hard as panicked pigeons crashed against the bars of their cage prisons, crying and pleading for their lives.

'Silence!' Fienne screeched. 'You're going to alert Reginald Grimster!'

The pigeons sank back in their cages.

I turned to see a pigeon standing next to us. 'This is Agent Swan,' Fienne said.

'Just call me Swan,' she said.

'Swan?'

'Don't ask,' Fienne whispered. 'She's a Stielbacht pigeon but her parents were confused about what type of bird she was when she was born, apparently.'

I could see why. Swan's white feathers meant it was an easy mistake to make.

'Tell me everything,' I said.

'Top-secret—' Fienne started.

'I can't help if you don't tell me what's going on.'

Fienne looked off into the distance for a while, then turned back to me. 'I've decided it's time you knew the truth. There is something I need to tell you.' He pulled me close. 'I'm a pigeon secret agent.'

'So *that's* what that cuff is,' I said, pointing at his black ankle bracelet. 'I thought you were a homing pigeon.'

'Pah. Just a homing pigeon?' Fienne fanned out his wings. "This is clearly an elite-issue black leg band, designated only for the bravest of spies.'

He stuck out his foot at me, making sure I took a close look.

'And you're an agent too?' I asked Swan.

'Yes, but I'm no longer a field agent,' Swan chirped. 'I work behind the scenes. I gather information and decipher vending-machine codes when agents need emergency supplies of chocolate bars.'

Fienne wrapped his wing around Swan's shoulders. 'I'd still be pecking at the vending-machine glass if it wasn't for you.'

'Just doing my job.' She nodded proudly and then turned to me. 'Will you help us?'

'I don't understand,' I said. 'If you are both agents, why do you need me?'

'I have a small health issue which prevents me from working in the field,' Swan said, looking away. 'I poo when I'm nervous.'

'It's true,' Fienne said. 'She gives away our position.'

'That's how we got trapped,' Swan said, staring down at her feet.

'Hold on,' I squawked. 'You were trapped by Reginald Grimster?'

'He tricked us with a stale brioche.' Fienne fiddled with his feathers. 'Even secret agents get hungry,' he said. 'Swan revealed our position when she pooed on the windowsill.'

'He strung us up in that cage over there,' Swan continued, pointing to a cardboard box near the window. 'But Fienne managed to release us.'

'It's an agent's duty to escape,' Fienne said, puffing out his chest feathers.

'But Reginald Grimster came back,' interrupted Swan. 'He spotted the empty box and as I hid, he grabbed Fienne.'

'He tied me to the toilet flush as punishment for escaping.' Fienne's eyes narrowed.

'We need your help,' Swan pleaded. 'Fienne is too injured to do this on his own and I might put him in danger again.'

My head was spinning. Without Swan, Fienne needed me to save the pigeons – but what did I know about being a secret agent?

'You said you wanted to tell me something,' I reminded Fienne. 'What was it?'

He nodded. 'Before I let you help me,

there *is* something you should know about me. About my last partner.'

The pigeons settled in their cages as Fienne took us back to his first mission in India. He told us how he had done his training at I-PLOP (the International Police Legion of Pigeons) and had been posted in India, where he had fallen in love with the Humans of India. He said they fed him sweet masala milk from tiny steel cups every day, and torn pieces of spicy naan. He flew free down the streets, dodging speeding rickshaws in the sizzling sunshine.

'My first mission was to investigate Reginald Grimster,' Fienne said. 'Back then India was full of pigeons but they seemed to be mysteriously disappearing. Even as a rookie agent, I could spot a bad Human a mile off. Reginald Grimster stood out amongst the kind Humans, dressed head to toe in a plastic mac, despite the boiling weather.'

'Reginald Grimster had come to the attention of I-PLOP after one Agent Kottur spotted the Human trying to order pigeon soup at a samosa stand,' Swan said.

'Agent Kottur was my first partner,'

Fienne added. 'He was a civilian pigeon just like you, but I saw great potential in him. I took him under my wing and trained him myself.' Fienne's head dropped. 'But he became obsessed with Reginald Grimster, and the mission cost Agent Kottur his life.'

I gasped. 'Reginald Grimster killed him?'

'Sorry, I meant "beak", not "life".'

'What happened?'

'Kottur flew straight into a freshly cleaned window whilst out on a mission to track Reginald Grimster.' Fienne sighed. 'He permanently bent his beak, and had to retire from I-PLOP.' Fienne straightened up. 'I promised Agent Kottur

I would finish the mission. I need to put an end to Reginald Grimster's pigeon crimes.'

'I understand,' I said.

Fienne held my shoulders. 'Are you sure you still want to help, even now you know what happened to my last partner?'

'Of course,' I said. 'Reginald Grimster needs to be stopped.'

'Yes, he does,' Fienne said, glaring at the door.

'You said he wanted to turn us pigeons into nuggets. Why?' I asked, scared to hear the answer. 'Why does he hate pigeons so much?'

'Years ago, he was pooed on by a pigeon,' said Swan. 'Ever since then he has wanted revenge.'

'Pigeons poo on Humans all the time!' I cried. 'But they don't all want to turn us into nuggets.'

'Have you noticed he has umbrellas on his shoulders for protection?' Fienne said. 'When he was pooed on all those years ago, his school friends made fun of him and started calling him Shoulder Poo.'

I giggled. 'That's pigeontastic.'

'I know.' Fienne sniggered. 'He hated being called Shoulder Poo.'

Skipper, There's no time for chuckling. My life is in danger!

'Your friend Dave is the one he intends to cook first,' Fienne said.

'How do you know?'

'Because he's in the *fattening* room.'

'The feed room?'

'The fattening room.' Fienne looked away. 'I lost my grandparents to a pie after they were taken to a fattening room.' He whipped his head back in my direction and stared at me. The orange of his eyes was bright and desperate. 'I need your help. You need to help me free these birds.'

He shuffled to the side of the room and picked up a piece of paper, shoving it towards me.

The Grimster Family ~~Chicken~~ Pigeon Nuggets Recipe

Ingredients:

- Chicken
- Some flour (or a sunflower)
- Beaten eggs (don't worry about taking the shells off, especially if you like your nuggets crunchy)
- Breadcrumbs
- Oil

What to do:

Preheat your oven. Whack it right up.

Cut chicken into pieces.

Dip the chicken into flour, then into eggs and finally into breadcrumbs. If you can't be bothered to do this, just go to a shop and buy some nuggets.

Brush the nuggets with oil and bake in the oven until they are just a tiny bit burnt but not too burnt.

If they're too burnt, make some more.

My stomach felt like it had just been punched. There was no doubt about it. Dave was going to be nuggeted.

8
The Fattening Room

'You need to help me unlock the cages,' Fienne said. 'Will you accept this mission, Skipper?'

I stood tall and puffed out my chest feathers. I realised I *could* help. I'd seen the keys to the birdcages near the cookbooks.

'I think I know where the keys are.'

Fienne grabbed me. 'Where?'

I looked around the room at the terrified pigeons. 'I will rescue you, Pigeon's Promise,' I called up to the crowd of imprisoned birds. 'But I need to help my friend first.'

I turned back to Fienne. 'If you help me save Dave, I'll get you the keys.'

Fienne nodded. 'Let's go.'

Swan listened out for Reginald Grimster, who was now in the garden, talking to someone again on his phone. She waved her wing, giving us the signal to leave.

Me and Fienne swooped down the stairs, straight to the fattening room.

'So you're back?' Dave said, smirking as he spotted me.

'Dave, this is important,' I said. 'You are in serious danger. Reginald Grimster plans to turn you into pigeon nuggets, and he's going to eat you!'

'WHAT?!'

'It's true, Dave. You have to believe me.'

'Why would a Human want to eat a pigeon?' asked Dave, raising his eyes to the ceiling. 'This is the most catbrained thing you've ever said.'

'I found a room full of trapped pigeons!' I shrieked, shaking my disbelieving friend by the shoulders.

'Where's this room? Where are all these pigeons?' Dave scoffed. 'Show me proof.'

Fienne stepped out from behind me.

'Who is that?' Dave said, shielding as much birdseed from Fienne as he could.

'He's Fienne,' I said.

'I don't care how he is,' Dave said. 'Who is he?'

'Fienne,' I cried. 'He's Fienne!'

'Yes. But who is he?'

'For Pigeon's sake,' Fienne interrupted. 'My name is Fienne. It's spelled F-I-E-N-N-E.'

'Ah,' Dave said. 'Why didn't you just say that?'

'None of that matters,' I cried, flapping my wings in Dave's face. 'You need to listen to him.'

'What Skipper said was correct,' said Fienne. 'Reginald Grimster is evil.'

'Don't be ridiculous,' Dave said. 'Just now he came through and complimented me on my plump bottom.'

'I found a chicken nugget recipe,' I hissed, waving the paper at Dave.

'Thank Pigeon,' Dave said, laughing. 'It's a *chicken* nugget recipe, Skipper. Not *pigeon* nugget. You can't make chicken nuggets from a pigeon.'

'*He* can!'

'Chicken nuggets *have* to be made from chickens. Not pigeons.' Dave shook his head. 'Otherwise they don't have that succulent chickeny flavour.'

'But didn't you say in the last book that pigeons taste like chicken?'

'Did I?'

'You did.'

Dave stopped. His eyes widened. 'There's only one thing we can do then.'

'Exactly,' I screeched. 'We need to get out of here—'

'And find a bookshop, get the book, come straight back here before we miss the late-afternoon feeding, and then read exactly what I said about pigeons tasting like chicken.'

'Dave! We don't have time for that.'

'How sure was I about us tasting like chicken?' he said, the feathers above his eyes furrowing.

'Very sure.'

Dave looked from me to Fienne and back to me again. The deep grey of his face started to pale.

A door slammed somewhere near the back of the house, shaking the walls of the fattening room. The stomp of Reginald Grimster's boots coming towards us grew louder and louder.

Dave gawked at me, his eyes wide and terrified.

'Then why are we standing around talking about books?' he panicked. 'We need to get out of here!'

Are you crying, Dave?'

No. I'm just really into this story.

9
Dave the Test Pigeon

'Hide,' Fienne hissed, shoving me down under the grains of birdseed. He pushed and pushed as we sank down, like pigeon eggs disappearing deep into a playground sandpit. Birdseed filled my beak as I wrestled to make a tiny vent in the piles of feed so I could breathe.

I heard Reginald Grimster pound across the dining room and into the fattening room. He was on the phone again. 'Hess, hmer,' he said. 'Aha. Hup. Hum. Hup. Hmmhmm. Hof morrrse.'

'He just said that he's going to take Dave to a supermarket,' Fienne mumbled through the darkness under the seed. 'Dave is to be the test pigeon.'

'How. Do. You. Know. That?' I asked, trying not to swallow birdseed each time I opened my beak.

'I learnt to decipher muffled Human at I-PLOP.'

'Hem-mem-memt. Himp him-mum him heery hat.'

'What did he say now?' I said.

'He said Dave will be the perfect test pigeon on account of how fat he is.'

'Help me, Skipper!' I heard Dave shriek as Reginald Grimster shushed him and slammed the door of a cage shut.

Then there was silence.

Suddenly a beak pecked through the piles of birdseed above my head, and I blinked as shards of light blinded me. Fienne pulled me up and flapped off the grains of birdseed trapped under my feathers. 'We need to go – NOW!'

We took flight. The front door slammed shut and we shot towards it. Through the glass panel in the door, I saw Dave being piled into the passenger seat of a rusty red car. He caught my eye and bashed at the cage with his wing just as Reginald Grimster started the car and set off down the road.

'Follow that car,' Fienne yelled at me.
'Where are the keys for the cages?'

My mind went blank. All I could think
about was Dave. I needed to get to Dave.

'The keys, Skipper!' Fienne screeched. 'Where are the keys?'

'I can't remember!'

'Think,' he said urgently. 'Think hard!'

Was it the kitchen? Or did I see them in the bathroom?

'Think quicker, Skipper,' Fienne yelled. 'Dave is on the way to being nuggeted.'

The cookbooks!

'The dining room!' I shrieked back. 'I remember I saw keys on the cupboard shelf, above the cookbooks.'

Fienne tapped the top of his head with his wing in a salute, and I raced upstairs and took off out of the bathroom window. I tore across the sky, chasing the red car and the evil Human who had birdnapped

my friend. Fat drops of rain started to fall as the skies turned grey and thunder rumbled. I sped through the hard rain after Dave.

The car went straight through the traffic lights, spraying a wave of puddle water right over a family waiting for a bus. Reginald Grimster veered left up a hill before turning right into the car park of a huge supermarket. It was one Dave and I had been to many times before. They had a pigeontastic doughnut aisle.

As the car parked up, I swooped down behind the Little Human boat ride near the front entrance. I watched as Reginald Grimster dragged a trolley across to his car. He pulled the back door open and reached in. Metal bars clanged as he dumped Dave's cage into the trolley. He then bent across the back seat of the car and pulled out a huge metal contraption with levers and clocks. He gently placed it next to Dave's cage, swung the car door shut and pushed the trolley past me and into the supermarket.

A Human Mum was on her way in with her Little Human in a buggy. I jumped into the basket in the bottom of the pushchair and curled up as small as I could, all the while watching the yellow plastic trousers in front of me.

Both trolleys went straight through the fruit and vegetable aisle and set off towards the back of the store. The Human Mum turned left, heading towards the refrigerators. I jumped out just in time to see Reginald Grimster roll Dave into a lift nearer the back. The doors shut and above the lift a number 1 lit up.

How was I supposed to get up now?

The next-door lift pinged open. I sped over and flew in. A Human Lady joined me and I did my best to look like a pigeon who was meant to be heading to the first floor.

As the lift arrived and the doors slid open, I spotted Reginald Grimster wheeling the trolley along a carpeted corridor towards a glass-walled office, where two Humans wearing very posh suits were sitting at a huge table. One had no hair and his bald head caught the light, almost blinding me.

I hopped out into the corridor, looking for a place to hide. Up above me the ceiling was lined with polystyrene tiles. One was broken. I flew up and squeezed through the crack, pecking my way across the foam surface until I was in the space above the first-floor offices. I cooed urgently to Dave and immediately heard him coo back. Following his call, I clambered across the tiles, until I was sure I was on top of the

right room, then I poked a small hole through the ceiling. Beneath me, Reginald Grimster, in all his yellow plastic mac fiendishness, was putting my caged, trembling friend on the desk.

The following chapters contain frightening scenes of pigeons in danger. If you are a pigeon of a nervous nature, grab a friend or an iced bun and hug them close.

10
Pigeon Poo Tastes Like Gone-off Milk (with Bits in It)

'Don't I know you?' one of the suited Humans said to Reginald Grimster.

Reginald Grimster's face turned red. 'Err—'

'Yes, I do know you!' the Human Man squealed. 'We went to school together.'

'You must be mistaken—'

'It's Reginald Grimster, isn't it?'

'Erm . . . yes . . .'

The Human Man sniggered and nudged his bald friend in the seat next to him. 'We were in PE once and a pigeon did a poo on his shoulder.' He turned to Reginald. 'What did we use to call you? Poo Face, wasn't it? Or was it Neck Poo?'

'Shoulder Poo,' Reginald Grimster growled through gritted teeth.

'That's right!' The Man slapped his thigh and laughed again, leaning back into his chair. 'We even had a song, didn't we? How did it go?'

'Shoulder Poo, Shoulder Poo, you got a shoulder poo-ooo,' Reginald Grimster said, his voice tiny as he glared at Dave. As the Human Man laughed and wiped tears from his eyes, Reginald Grimster mouthed the words 'I hate pigeons' at Dave.

'Need some help?' Fienne landed suddenly next to me.

'Fienne! Thank Pigeon you're here.'

'Where's Dave?'

'He's trapped down there!' I pointed to the hole in the ceiling.

'I want to see,' came a voice from behind Fienne.

'Who's that?'

A patter of feet landed around me and Fienne, and suddenly the space above the

117

ceiling was filled with pigeons.

'They wanted to help,' Fienne said, shrugging.

'Can I see?' Swan asked, pushing under my wing.

'Swan! What are you doing here?' I said as she nodded at me. 'I thought you didn't do fieldwork?'

'You were so brave to help all these pigeons, Skipper,' she said. 'It was only right I did my bit.'

'If she gets to see, I want to see too,' came another voice.

'And me!'

Pigeons clambered all over each other trying to reach the tiny hole in the ceiling tile. They pushed and shoved and bundled in on top of me and Fienne.

Plop.

'What was that?' I asked.

'Oh no!' Swan's white feathers around her beak started to turn pink. 'I think I did a poo.'

We looked down and saw a white blob floating in the teacup next to Reginald Grimster's old school friend.

We watched as he picked up the cup and took a sip of tea. He shuddered, twisting his lips over his teeth. 'This tea tastes a bit funny.'

'The milk must have gone off,' the bald Human Man said.

The school friend looked into his cup and swirled it around. 'But there's bits in it.'

I turned to Swan, who looked horrified. 'I didn't mean to,' she said. 'You know it happens when I get nervous.'

'Silence, everyone,' Fienne whistled. 'I can't hear what's going on down there.'

'Perhaps we should move on to why you are here,' the bald Man said to Reginald Grimster. 'What's in the trolley?'

The Human Men sat up and eyed the

machine. Reginald Grimster's angry eyebrows relaxed as he pulled out the metal construction and placed it delicately on the table.

'This here is Reginald Grimster's pride and joy.' Reginald Grimster beamed. 'It's the first-ever, one-of-a-kind, Official (Unofficial) Pigeon Nugget Maker,' he said proudly. 'And it's going to make us millionaires.'

'Pigeon nuggets?' said the old school friend Human, his eyebrows shooting up to his forehead.

'Yup,' Reginald Grimster said. 'They taste just like chicken nuggets, but they're much cheaper to make because there are hundreds of pigeons wandering around, so you don't need to spend money buying birds.'

'It sounds disgusting,' the bald Man grumbled.

'It's not!' Reginald Grimster snapped. 'And Reginald Grimster has brought a pigeon here to show you. This machine will pluck him, mince him, cook him and nugget him, and all you have to do is press this button and wait three minutes.' He pointed to a big red button at the top of the device.

Reginald Grimster then unlocked the cage door and pulled Dave out with a gloved hand. He clasped him tightly and slowly unscrewed a metal cap on the top of the machine. He smiled widely as he lifted off the lid. Dave screeched,

'HELP ME!'

11
It's Raining Pigeons

'What are you doing?!' the Human Men shouted, horrified.

'Reginald Grimster is going to make pigeon nuggets.'

'You can't mince a pigeon in here!' the bald Man bellowed. 'What's wrong with you, Shoulder Poo?!'

Reginald Grimster's eyes narrowed. 'Reginald Grimster has come to make pigeon nuggets, and Reginald Grimster WILL MAKE pigeon nuggets.' He pressed the huge red button.

Dave screamed as the Pigeon Nugget Maker whirred into life. A plunger started to move up and down inside as the blades at the base of the machine began to slice faster and faster. 'Skipper, help me!' Dave shrieked.

'I'm coming!' I squawked down.

I pecked at the foam tile as hard as I could, but it was too thick. I scraped with my claws and stabbed at the floor beneath me, trying to get into the room.

The bald Man sprang out of his seat and clambered across the desk, grabbing for the machine. 'Oh no you don't!'

'Your Medal of the Brave, Dave!' I screamed down. 'Throw your medal!'

Dave flung the shiny bottle top off his

chest. Time seemed to slow as we both watched the medal tumble through the air towards the open top of the machine. It hit the rim and bounced across to the other side before circling like a gobstopper on a basketball hoop. For a moment, the medal stood still.

And then it fell in.

The Pigeon Nugget Maker started to shake as the bald Man and Reginald Grimster, still grasping Dave tight, battled for it. The whirring and the chomping grew louder and louder. Smoke spilled out of the top as the machine was rammed back and forth between the fighting Humans. Dave was squashed against the machine, bashing at Reginald Grimster, trying to scratch and claw himself free from the Human's grip.

The blades stopped suddenly as the contraption jerked to a halt – and the smell of molten metal poured out of the Nugget Maker.

Reginald Grimster pushed the bald Man away as he hugged his beloved machine and let out a cry. Dave stumbled to an empty space on the desk as Reginald Grimster started to fiddle with the levers and dials.

Crack.

'What's that cracking sound?' I squawked, trying to get a better view of Dave.

Pigeons shoved forwards, pushing against me as we all tried to peer out of the tiny hole.

Craaack.

'*That!*' I said. 'What is that?'

'It wasn't me this time,' Swan said.

'Hold on,' Fienne crowed at the pigeons
gathering upon us. 'If too many of
you come at once, we'll all collapse
right through the ceiling—'

Crrrraaaaaaaaack!

'Too late!'

The foam tile split and
we all tumbled through the
hole and into the glass room.

'What on Earth!' the Human Men
screamed.

Pigeons rained through the ceiling,
bouncing off the table and the walls and the
floor. Feathers flew and claws scraped at

the glass as we tried to grab on to anything to break our fall.

'There's a pigeon in my hair!' one Human roared.

'There's a pigeon down my pants!' the other one yelled.

'THEY ARE POOING ON MY NECK!'

Reginald Grimster stared up, his eyes wide in terror. He flicked up his shoulder umbrellas. Me and Fienne flew towards

Dave. I landed on the machine and kicked my way over to him. Fienne beat his wings in Reginald Grimster's face, protecting my injured friend.

'Come on, Dave!' I screeched.

Dave pushed himself up. 'My medal!'

He charged at Reginald Grimster and the Nugget Maker. Fienne beat his wings harder as Reginald Grimster tried to bat him away. Dave dived into the machine and yanked out his charred medal with his beak. I gripped his head with my feet, pulling him out.

'NO! Get back in there, pigeon!' Reginald Grimster snarled. He smacked Fienne out of the way and bent over the machine, grabbing at Dave.

'The red button!' Fienne cawed.

'My pleasure,' Dave said, using all his might to kick it as we flew past.

The machine buzzed and hummed and whirred back to life.

'WAIT!' Reginald cried as his glued-on hair fell into the Nugget Maker.

The machine juddered and shook. Smoke poured out of the chomping base as the smell of burning hair filled the glass room. We all watched as the contraption whistled louder and louder, rocking back and forward, jumping up with every judder.

Pieces of metal flew out in every direction. Levers dropped off and clocks span up into the air.

Then it stopped, and out shot a burnt
nugget of fake hair.

'My hair!' Reginald Grimster wailed,
picking up the shrivelled, blackened ball.

He looked up at the ceiling in despair,
just as a blob of white dropped through the
air and landed right between his eyebrows.

'So sorry,' said Swan, hovering by me.
'It always happens when I'm nervous.'

12
FLY!

'Get back here, you disgusting pigeons!'

Reginald Grimster swept the poo off his face with his hand. His face went from red to purple as he picked up a broken lever and charged at us.

'Time to go!' Fienne shrieked at us. The

other Humans had obviously decided the same thing, as they ran for the door and threw it open. We all rushed after them.

Dave flapped as hard as he could, but couldn't stay in flight for long because of his bad wing. Reginald Grimster grabbed at him, yanking him away from us. Fienne dived down and beaked the evil Human right between the eyes.

'That's for Agent Kottur!' he yelled.

Reginald Grimster howled, clutching his plucked eyebrows and accidentally lobbing Dave over his head. Fienne caught Dave between his legs and dashed at the door.

'COME BACK HERE!' Reginald Grimster snarled, running after us. 'NO PIGEON GETS THE BETTER OF REGINALD GRIMSTER!'

Pigeons tore down the corridor, racing towards the opening lift doors. Feathered bodies tumbled in, filling the space. Fienne soared high and flung Dave in after the others, and grabbing my leg, pulled me in after him.

'Hit the down button!' Dave screeched at the pigeon next to the lift controls.

'Which one is the down button?!' the pigeon squawked back.

'Hit anything!' Swan cried.

Every number on the panel lit up as pigeons headbutted whatever button they could. The doors started to close. Reginald Grimster dived at the lift. The doors slammed shut just as Reginald Grimster's face thudded against the metal and the lift slowly jerked into action.

'We made it!' Dave cried.

'Not quite,' Fienne said, pointing at a tiny yellow shoulder umbrella stuck between the doors.

'Noooo!' Reginald Grimster yelled as the lift moved, dragging him down. 'Ow!' he groaned as he thudded against the floor on the other side of the doors.

Fienne held down a button and the lift started to judder down again.

'Not again,' Reginald Grimster moaned. 'Ouch,' he cried as he was pulled flat against the floor.

The tiny umbrella tore free, leaving Reginald Grimster on the first floor, and the lift took us down to the ground floor. The doors slid open and we swooped out into the supermarket.

'AHHHH!'

Humans screamed and shrieked. They ducked beneath shelves and hid under fruit crates. Little Humans danced and clapped their hands, cheering us on. For a moment, hundreds of pigeons turned the supermarket grey and feathery and it was glorious.

Fienne nodded at me as Dave and I watched him make sure every pigeon got out of the lift safely. Swan waved us goodbye as she escorted the pigeons out of the shop.

'It was good to work with you,' Fienne said, saluting me.

'And you too,' I said. 'Thanks for everything.'

'We're always looking for new recruits at I-PLOP, if you are interested?' Fienne asked. 'You'd get to travel the world and visit the wondrous India.'

It might have been because we were standing in the World Foods aisle, but I could almost smell the scent of spicy cinnamon in sweetened masala milk. And it might've been because the chicken rotisserie was on behind us, but I could almost feel the balminess of the hot Indian summer evenings through my feathers. The thought of crisp fennel seeds on naan bread made me feel warm inside.

Then I looked at Dave, who was

struggling to stick his medal back on his chest. His tail was crushed and the Nugget Machine had left long scratches on his back and feet.

'I think I'll have to say no,' I said.

'I understand,' said Fienne. 'You are a good friend.' He ushered out the last pigeon from the lift and dropped the broken shoulder umbrella into a nearby bin. 'Dave,' he said, saluting my friend.

'Fienne,' Dave said, his head bobbing back.

'Will we see you again?' I asked.

'Top-secret pigeon business, I'm afraid.'

He glided up into the air and followed the other pigeons out of the store (the ones who weren't in the unattended doughnut aisle, anyway).

Me and Dave jumped into the hood of a Little Human heading towards the door on a scooter and hitched a ride to the car park.

'I should've believed you—' Dave started.

'It's OK,' I said. 'I shouldn't have left you.'

We hopped out as the Little Human skidded to a stop at the exit. The sky was turning dark but the rain had eased. The lights in the shop windows glowed yellow in the darkness and made the puddles twinkle.

That's when I caught a whiff of leaf-blower engine oil and premium canary food.

'Look over there,' I said to Dave, as we gazed across the rows of cars. 'It's Him Next Door!'

13
Home Sweet Jammy Biscuit Home

As Him Next Door filled his car with shopping, we clambered in through an open window and hid in the passenger footwell. We listened to his terrible singing all the way home, as he warbled along to the radio.

I could hear Dave breathe a huge sigh of relief as Him Next Door pulled up alongside our Human Lady's house. There was something about being home that felt like discovering an abandoned ice cream cart on a warm summer's day. We jumped out of the car, while Him Next Door unloaded the bags from the boot and padded across the lawn towards the Human Lady's house. He noticed us and came over, his hand filled with broken biscuit bits from a packet of digestives in one of his shopping bags.

'You're the pigeons from the shed, aren't you?' he said.

We nodded.

'Well, you look like the pigeons from the shed,' he said, clearly not understanding our nod. 'Don't you worry, little guys. She'll be back from her holiday in a few days.'

'She's coming back!' Dave cooed at me. 'I knew she wouldn't leave us!'

We gobbled up the crumbs from Him Next Door and watched him head back across the front lawn towards his home. Then we scrambled around the side of the house and into the back garden.

'You don't suppose she'll come back without Mean Cat, do you?' Dave asked hopefully.

'I think she'll be back *with* Mean Cat,' I said. 'She loves that catbrained furball.'

Dave sighed. 'Oh well. I suppose it could

be worse. One Mean Cat is better than being nuggeted.'

'Think of all the delicious biscuits and bread,' I said back. 'One Mean Cat is better than a lifetime of birdseed.'

Dave nodded. 'And at least she only has one cat,' he said. 'One Mean Cat is definitely better than two Mean Cats.'

And he's right. But that's a story for another time.

14
The End of the Book

This really is the end of the book. There's no more story left. The end.

I'm not kidding. It's The Actual End.

(The endy endy end end endy endy end. Endy endy endy endy endy endy end.)

THE END.

End end end end end end end end end end end end end end end end end end end

end end end end end end end end end end
end end end end end end end end end end
end end end end end end end end end end
end end end end end end end end end end
end end end end end end end end end end
end end end end end end end end end end
end end end end end end end end end end
end end end end end end end end end end
end end end end end end end end end end
end end end end end end end end end end
end end end end end end end end end end
end end end end end end end end end end
end end end end end end end end end end
end end end end end end end end end end
end end end end end end end end end end
end end end end end end end end end end
end end end end end end end end end end

end end end end end end end end end end
end end end end end end end end end end
end end end end end end end end end end
end end end end end end end end end end
end end end end end end end end end end
end end end end end end end end end end
end end end end end end end end end end
end end end end end end end end end end
end end end end end end end end end end
end end end end end end end end end end
end end end end end end end end end end
end end end end end end end end end end
end end end end end end end end end end
end end end end end end end end end end
end end end end end end end end end end
end end end end end end end end end end
end end end end end end end end end end

end end end end end end end end end end
end end end end end end end end end end
end end end end end end end end end end
end end end end end end end end end end
end end end end end end end end end end
end end end end end end end end end end
end end end end end end end end end end
end end end end end end end end end end
end end end end end end end end end end
end end end end end end end end end end
end end end end end end end end end end
end end end end end end end end end end
end end end end end end end end end end
end end end end end end end end end end
end end end end end end end end end end
end end end end end end end end end end
end end end end end end end end end end

end end end end end end end end end end

end end end end end end end end end end

end end end end end end end end end end

end end end end end end end end end end

end end end end end end end end end end

end end end end end end end end end end

end end end end end end end end end end

end end end end end end end end end end

end end end end end end end end end end

end end end end end end end end end end

end end end end end end enb end end end

end end end end end end end end end end

end end end end end end end end end end

end end end end end end end end end end

end end end end end end end end end end

end end end end end end end end end end

end end end end end end end end end end

end end end end end end end end end end
end end end end end end end end end end
end.

The six hundred and thirty-sixth 'end' actually says 'enb'. Sorry about that; my wing got stuck on the B key.

The Bit After the End
What's your pigeon name?

Take the last letter off your first name.

Now add it back on.

That's your pigeon name.

DAVE
Pigeon
The best book you'll ever read!
How to Deal with Bad Cats and Keep (most of) Your Feathers
SWAPNA HADDOW
Illustrated by Sheena Dempsey

Can't get enough of Dave
and Skipper?

Here's a sneaky peek of
their first adventure . . .

1

The Beginning of *This* Story Instead

Dave and me were on a routine croissant heist. It was something we'd done at least a hundred times before.

In fact, the first time I met Dave was on a croissant heist. Back then, Dave told me he had just won a Medal of the Brave which he wore all the time. (Though I

heard a rumour later it was just a bottle
top that had got stuck to him with a piece
of chewing gum when he got caught in a
bin bag once).

Dave was swooping in from the
opposite side of the pond when we
both spotted a half-eaten croissant
abandoned under a bench. We
dived down, crashing towards the
same gap between two planks of
bench wood, and landed at the exact
same time.

There we were, dangling upside down,
stuck in the bench, when a huge goose
grabbed our croissant and waddled off
with it. A goose, for Bird's sake.

We never did get that croissant back, did we?
Dave!
What?
Do you want me to tell this story?
Sorry, Skipper. On you go.

What I was about to say was – we never got our croissant back. We caught up to the goose just fine, but let me tell you something about geese. They are far bigger up close than when you see them in the distance. And they are very pecky. We were grateful to leave that fight with all our feathers.

Dave and I have been friends ever since.

Have you got to the bit where I almost lost my life?

Can you stop interrupting me?! I was just about to start that bit, but you keep ruining the story by giving things away!

Where was I? Ah, yes. The day we met Mean Cat. Our one hundredth croissant heist.

It was a bright, sunny morning, and me and Dave were starving. Peck-your-own-feathers-off starving. All we'd had for breakfast were the wet breadcrumbs a Little Human had already chewed and spat out, and a teeny-tiny piece of an iced bun we'd managed to steal from a duck.

That's when I spotted a Human Lady. We couldn't believe our luck. Everyone knows that Human Ladies like to carry around crusts with them. Dave said that's what their handbags were for.

Dave and I pattered over trying to look friendly and hungry.

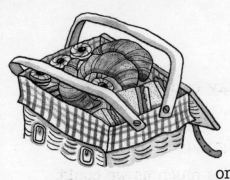

As predicted, the Human Lady popped the clasp on her picnic basket. There was more than just bread! Inside we spied a feast of croissants, sandwiches and biscuits. And they were the biscuits with the jam in the middle. My favourites.

'Follow me,' I said, shuffling closer.

The Human Lady spotted us. 'Good morning.'

We didn't say anything back because we couldn't speak Human.

'Would you like some croissant?' she said.

Of course we would.

She read our minds and tore off a piece

of golden-brown flaky pastry, throwing it towards us.

The sweet crumbs tumbled to our feet and we gobbled up as much as we could, filling our aching bellies. We inched closer to the basket, hoping to pinch a pastry or two for supper later.

'You two must be hungry,' the Human Lady said, throwing us broken bits of bread.

Dave cooed and hopped even closer to the basket. 'Come on,' he said, nodding at me.

I caught a whiff of something awful. 'What's that?'

'What?'

'That smell . . .'

'Sorry,' said Dave, fanning his bottom. 'I think it's that biryani from the bin I had last night.'

'Not *that* smell—'

The stink got stronger and stronger, burning my nostrils and stinging my eyes.

'Stop!' the Human Lady shouted. *'Stop!'*

A flash of ginger and white shot out from behind the basket. Sharp needles scratched my feathers.

The fiery stench of grass and wee meant only one thing. Cat.

Claws stung my back. I ran fast, took off and flapped for my life. Down below, I could see shiny strands of spit stretched across sharp fangs, as the orange ball of fur leapt after me, hungry for a bite. . .

Watch out for more
Dave Pigeon
adventures,
Coming Soon!